LOST ART

George O. Smith

Pharos Books

ISBN: 978-93-55467-06-5
eISBN: 978-93-55467-11-9

©Publisher

Publisher: Pharos Books (P) Ltd.
Plot No.-55, Main Mother Dairy Road
Pandav Nagar, East Delhi-110092
Phone: 011-40395855, +4049916623
WhatsApp: +91 8368220032
E-mail: sales@pharosbooks.in
Website: www.pharosbooks.in
First Edition: 2023

LOST ART
By George O. Smith

LOST ART

Sargon of Akkad was holding court in all of his splendor in the Mesopotamia area, which he thought to be the center of the Universe. The stars to him were but holes in a black bowl which he called the sky. They were beautiful then, as they are now, but he thought that they were put there for his edification only; for was he not the ruler of Akkadia?

After Sargon of Akkad, there would come sixty centuries of climbing before men reached the stars and found not only that there had been men upon them, but that a civilization on Mars had reached its peak four thousand years before Christ and was now but a memory and a wealth of pictographs that adorned the semipreserved Temples of Canalopsis.

And sixty centuries after, the men of Terra wondered about the ideographs and solved them sufficiently to piece together the wonders of the long-dead Martian Civilization.

Sargon of Akkad did not know that the stars that he beheld carried on them wonders his mind would not, could not, accept.

Altas, the Martian, smiled tolerantly at his son. The young man boasted on until Altas said: "So you have memorized the contents of my manual? Good, Than, for I am growing old and I would be pleased to have my son fill my shoes. Come into the workshop that I may pass upon your proficiency."

Altas led Than to the laboratory that stood at the foot of the great tower of steel; Altas removed from a cabinet a replacement element from the great beam above their heads, and said: "Than, show me how to hook this up!"

Than's eyes glowed. From other cabinets he took small auxiliary parts. From hooks upon the wall, Than took lengths of wire. Working with a brilliant deftness that was his heritage as a Martian, Than spent an hour attaching the complicated circuits. After he was finished, Than stepped back and said: "There—and believe it or not, this is the first time you have permitted me to work with one of the beam elements."

"You have done well," said Altas with that same cryptic smile. "But now we shall see. The main question is: Does it work?"

"Naturally," said Than in youthful pride. "Is it not hooked up exactly as your manual says? It will work."

"We shall see," repeated Altas. "We shall see."

Barney Carroll and James Baler cut through the thin air of Mars in a driver-wing flier at a terrific rate of speed. It was the only kind of flier that would work on Mars with any degree of safety since it depended upon the support of its drivers rather than the wing surface. They were hitting it up at almost a thousand miles per hour on their way from Canalopsis to Lincoln Head; their trip would take an hour and a half.

As they passed over the red sand of Mars, endlessly it seemed, a glint of metal caught Barney's eye, and he shouted.

"What's the matter, Barney?" asked Jim.

"Roll her over and run back a mile or so," said Barney. "I saw something down there that didn't belong in this desert."

Jim snapped the plane around in a sharp loop that nearly took their heads off, and they ran back along their course.

"Yop," called Barney, "there she is!"

"What?"

"See that glint of shiny metal? That doesn't belong in this mess of erosion. Might be a crash."

"Hold tight," laughed Jim. "We're going down."

They did. Jim's piloting had all of the aspects of a daredevil racing pilot's, and Barney was used to it. Jim snapped the nose of the little flier down and they power-dived to within a few yards of the sand before he set the plane on its tail and skidded flatwise to kill speed. He leveled off, and the flier came screaming in for a perfect landing not many feet from the glinting object.

"This is no crash," said Baler. "This looks like the remains of an air-lane beacon of some sort."

"Does it? Not like any I've ever seen. It reminds me more of some of the gadgets they find here and there—the remnants of the Ancients. They used to build junk like this."

"Hook up the sand-blower," suggested Jim Baler. "We'll clear some of this rubble away and see what she really looks like. Can't see much more than what looks like a high-powered searchlight."

Barney hauled equipment out of the flier and hitched it to a small motor in the plane. The blower created a small storm for an hour or so, its blast directed by suit-clad Barney Carroll. Working with experience gained in uncovering the remains of a dozen dead and buried cities, Barney cleared the shifting sand from the remains of the tower.

The head was there, preserved by the dry sand. Thirty feet below the platform, the slender tower was broken off. No delving could find the lower portion.

"This is quite a find," said Jim. "Looks like some of the carvings on the Temple of Science at Canalopsis—that little house on the top of the spire with the three-foot runway around it; then this dingbat perched on top of the roof. Never did figure out what it was for."

"We don't know whether the Martians' eyes responded as ours do," suggested Barney. "This might be a searchlight that puts out with Martian visible spectrum. If they saw with infrared, they wouldn't be using Terran fluorescent lighting. If they saw with long heat frequencies, they wouldn't waste power with even a tungsten filament light, but would have invented something that cooked its most energy in the visible spectrum, just as we have in the last couple of hundred years."

"That's just a guess, of course."

"Naturally," said Barney. "Here, I've got the door cracked. Let's be the first people in this place for six thousand years Terran. Take it easy, this floor is at an angle of thirty degrees."

"I won't slide. G'wan in. I'm your shadow."

They entered the thirty-foot circular room and snapped on their torches. There was a bench that ran almost around the entire room. It was empty save for a few scraps of metal and a Martian book of several hundred metal pages.

"Nuts," said Barney, "we would have to find a thing like this but empty. That's our luck. What's the book, Jim?"

"Some sort of text, I'd say. Full of diagrams and what seems to be mathematics. Hard to tell, of course, but we've established the fact that mathematics is universal, though the characters can not possibly be."

"Any chance of deciphering it?" asked Barney.

"Let's get back in the flier and try. I'm in no particular hurry."

"Nor am I. I don't care whether we get to Lincoln Head tonight or the middle of next week."

"Now let's see that volume of diagrams," he said as soon as they were established in the flier.

Jim passed the book over, and Barney opened the book to the first page. "If we never find anything else," he said, "this will make us famous. I am now holding the first complete volume of Martian literature that anyone has ever seen. The darned thing is absolutely complete, from cover to cover!"

"That's a find," agreed Jim. "Now go ahead and transliterate it— you're the expert on Martian pictographs."

For an hour, Barney scanned the pages of the volume. He made copious notes on sheets of paper which he inserted between the metal leaves of the book. At the end of that time, during which Jim Baler had been inspecting the searchlight-thing on the top of the little house, he called to his friend, and Jim entered the flier lugging the thing on his shoulders.

"What'cha got?" he grinned. "I brought this along. Nothing else in that shack, so we're complete except for the remnants of some very badly corroded cable that ran from this thing to a flapping end down where the tower was broken."

Barney smiled and blinked. It was strange to see this big man working studiously over a book; Barney Carroll should have been leading a horde of Venusian engineers through the Palanortis country instead of delving into the artifacts of a dead civilization.

"I think that this thing is a sort of engineer's handbook," he said. "In the front there is a section devoted to mathematical tables. You know, a table of logs to the base twelve which is because the Martians had six fingers on each hand. There is what seems to be a table of definite integrals—at least if I were writing a handbook I'd place the table of integrals at the last part of the math section. The geometry and trig is absolutely recognizable because of the designs. So is the solid geom and the analyt for the same reason. The next section seems to be devoted to chemistry; the Martians used a hexagonal figure for a benzene ring, too, and so that's established. From that we find the key to the Periodic Chart of the Atoms which is run vertically instead of horizontally, but still unique. These guys were sharp, though; they seem to have hit upon the fact that isotopes are separate elements though so close in grouping to one another that they exhibit the same properties. Finding this will uncover a lot of mystery."

"Yeah," agreed Baler, "from a book of this kind we can decipher most anything. The keying on a volume of physical constants is perfect and almost infinite in number. What do they use for Pi?"

"Circle with a double dot inside."

"And Planck's Constant?"

"Haven't hit that one yet. But we will. But to get back to the meat of this thing, the third section deals with something strange. It seems to have a bearing on this gadget from the top of the tower. I'd say that the volume was a technical volume on the construction, maintenance, and repair of the tower and its functions—whatever they are."

Barney spread the volume out for Jim to see. "That dingbat is some sort of electronic device. Or, perhaps subelectronic. Peel away that rusted side and we'll look inside."

Jim peeled a six-inch section from the side of the big metal tube, and they inspected the insides. Barney looked thoughtful for a minute and then flipped the pages of the book until he came to a diagram.

"Sure," he said exultantly, "this is she. Look, Jim, they draw a cathode like this, and the grids are made with a series of fine parallel lines. Different, but more like the real grid than our symbol of a zig-zag line. The plate is a round circle instead of a square, but that's so clearly defined that it comes out automatically. Here's your annular electrodes, and the ... call 'em deflection plates. I think we can hook this do-boodle up as soon as we get to our place in Lincoln Head."

"Let's go then. Not only would I like to see this thing work, but I'd give anything to know what it's for!"

"You run the crate," said Barney, "and I'll try to decipher this mess into voltages for the electrode-supply and so on. Then we'll be in shape to go ahead and hook her up."

The trip to Lincoln Head took almost an hour. Barney and Jim landed in their landing yards and took the book and the searchlight-thing inside. They went to their laboratory, and called for sandwiches and tea. Jim's sister brought in the food a little later and found them tinkering with the big beam tube.

"What have you got this time?" she groaned.

"Name it and it's yours," laughed Barney.

"A sort of gadget that we found on the Red Desert."

"What does it do?" asked Christine Baler.

"Well," said Jim, "it's a sort of a kind of a dingbat that does things."

"Uh-huh," said Christine. "A dololly that plings the inghams."

"Right!"

"You're well met, you two. Have your fun. But for Pete's sake don't forget to eat. Not that you will, I know you, but a girl has got to make some sort of attempt at admonishment. I'm going to the moom-picher. I'll see you when I return."

"I'd say stick around," said Barney. "But I don't think we'll have anything to show you for hours and hours. We'll have something by the time you return."

Christine left, and the men applied themselves to their problem. Barney had done wonders in unraveling the unknown. Inductances, he found, were spirals; resistance were dotted lines; capacitances were parallel squares.

"What kind of stuff do we use for voltages?" asked Jim.

"That's a long, hard trail," laughed Barney. "Basing my calculations on the fact that their standard voltage cell was the same as ours, we apply the voltages as listed on my schematic here."

"Can you assume that their standard is the same as ours?"

"Better," said Barney. "The Terran Standard Cell—the well-known Weston Cell—dishes out what we call 1.0183 volts at twenty degrees C. Since the Martian description of their Standard Cell is essentially the same as the Terran, they are using the same thing. Only they use sense and say that a volt is the unit of a standard cell, period. Calculating their figures on the numerical base of twelve is tricky, but I've done it."

"You're doing fine. How do you assume their standard is the same?"

"Simple," said Barney in a cheerful tone. "Thank God for their habit of drawing pictures. Here we have the well-known H tube. The electrodes are signified by the symbols for the elements used. The

Periodic Chart in the first section came in handy here. But look, master mind, this dinky should be evacuated, don't you think?"

"If it's electronic or subelectronic, it should be. We can solder up this breach here and apply the hyvac pump. Rig us up a power supply whilst I repair the blowout."

"Where's the BFO?"

"What do you want with that?" asked Jim.

"The second anode takes about two hundred volts worth of eighty-four cycles," explained Barney. "Has a sign that seems to signify 'In Phase,' but I'll be darned if I know with what. Y'know, Jim, this dingbat looks an awful lot like one of the drivers we use in our spaceships and driver-wing fliers."

"Yeah," drawled Jim. "About the same recognition as the difference between Edison's first electric light and a twelve-element, electron multiplier, power output tube. Similarity: They both have cathodes."

"Edison didn't have a cathode—"

"Sure he did. Just because he didn't hang a plate inside of the bottle doesn't stop the filament from being a cathode."

Barney snorted. "A monode, hey?"

"Precisely. After which come diodes, triodes, tetrodes, pentodes, hexodes, heptodes—"

"—and the men in the white coats. How's your patching job?"

"Fine. How's your power-supply job?"

"Good enough," said Barney. "This eighty-four cycles is not going to be a sine wave at two hundred volts; the power stage of the BFO overloads just enough to bring in a bit of second harmonic."

"A beat-frequency-oscillator was never made to run at that level," complained Jim Baler. "At least, not this one. She'll tick on a bit of second, I think."

"Are we ready for the great experiment?"

"Yup, and I still wish I knew what the thing was for. Go ahead, Barney. Crack the big switch!"

Altas held up a restraining hand as Than grasped the main power switch. "Wait," he said. "Does one stand in his sky flier and leave the ground at full velocity? Or does one start an internal combustion engine at full speed?"

"No," said the youngster. "We usually take it slowly."

"And like the others, we must tune our tube. And that we cannot do under full power. Advance your power lever one-tenth step and we'll adjust the deflection anodes."

"I'll get the equipment," said Than. "I forgot that part."

"Never mind the equipment," smiled Altas. "Observe."

Altas picked up a long screw-driverlike tool and inserted it into the maze of wiring that surrounded the tube. Squinting in one end of the big tube, he turned the tool until the cathode surface brightened slightly. He adjusted the instrument until the cathode was at its brightest, and then withdrew the tool.

"That will do for your experimental set-up," smiled Altas. "The operation in service is far more critical and requires equipment. As an experiment, conducted singly, the accumulative effect cannot be dangerous, though if the deflection plates are not properly served with their supply voltages, the experiment is a failure. The operation of the tube depends upon the perfection of the deflection-plate voltages."

"No equipment is required, then?"

"It should have been employed," said Altas modestly. "But in my years as a beam-tower attendant, I have learned the art of aligning the plates by eye. Now, son, we may proceed from there."

Barney Carroll took a deep breath and let the power switch fall home. Current meters swung across their scales for an instant, and then the lights went out in the house!

"Fuse blew," said Barney shortly. He gumbled his way through the dark house and replaced the fuse. He returned smiling. "Fixed that one," he told Jim. "Put a washer behind it."

"O.K. Hit the switch again."

Barney cranked the power over, and once more the meters climbed up across the scales. There was a groaning sound from the tube, and the smell of burning insulation filled the room. One meter blew with an audible sound as the needle hit the end stop, and immediately afterward the lights in the entire block went out.

"Fix that one by hanging a penny behind it," said Jim with a grin.

"That's a job for Martian Electric to do," laughed Barney.

Several blocks from there, an attendant in the substation found the open circuit-breaker and shoved it in with a grim smile. He looked up at the power-demand meter and grunted. High for this district, but not dangerous. Duration, approximately fifteen seconds. Intensity, higher than usual but not high enough to diagnose any failure of the wiring in the district. "Ah, well," he thought, "we can crank up the blow-point on this breaker if it happens again."

He turned to leave and the crashing of the breaker scared him out of a week's growth. He snarled and said a few choice words not fit for publication. He closed the breaker and screwed the blow-point control up by two-to-one. "That'll hold 'em," he thought, and then the ringing of the telephone called him to his office, and he knew that he was in for an explanatory session with some people who wanted to know why their lights were going on and off. He composed a plausible tale on his way to the phone. Meanwhile, he wondered about the unreasonable demand and concluded that one of the folks had just purchased a new power saw or something for their home workshop.

"Crack the juice about a half," suggested Barney. "That'll keep us on the air until we find out what kind of stuff this thing takes. The book claims about one tenth of the current-drain for this unit. Something we've missed, no doubt."

"Let's see that circuit," said Jim. After a minute, he said: "Look, guy, what are these screws for?"

"They change the side plate voltages from about three hundred to about three hundred and fifty. I've got 'em set in the middle of the range."

"Turn us on half voltage and diddle one of 'em."

"That much of a change shouldn't make the difference," objected Barney.

"Brother, we don't know what this thing is even for," reminded Jim. "Much less do we know the effect of anything on it. Diddle, I say."

"O.K., we diddle." Barney turned on half power and reached into the maze of wiring and began to tinker with one of the screws. "Hm-m-m," he said after a minute. "Does things, all right. She goes through some kind of resonance point or something. There is a spot of minimum current here. There! I've hit it. Now for the other one."

For an hour, Barney tinkered with first one screw and then the other one. He found a point where the minimum current was really low; the two screws were interdependent and only by adjusting them alternately was he able to reach the proper point on each. Then he smiled and thrust the power on full. The current remained at a sane value.

"Now what?" asked Barney.

"I don't know. Anything coming out of the business end?"

"Heat."

"Yeah, and it's about as lethal as a sun lamp. D'ye suppose the Martians used to artificially assist their crops by synthetic sunshine?"

Barney applied his eye to a spectroscope. It was one of the newer designs that encompassed everything from short ultraviolet to long infrared by means of fluorescent screens at the invisible wave lengths. He turned the instrument across the spectrum and shook his head. "Might be good for a chest cold," he said, "but you wouldn't get a sunburn off of it. It's all in the infra. Drops off like a cliff just below the deep red. Nothing at all in the visible or above. Gee," he said with a queer smile, "you don't suppose that they died off because of a pernicious epidemic of colds and they tried chest-cooking *en masse?*"

"I'd believe anything if this darned gadget were found in a populated district," said Jim. "But we know that the desert was here when the Martians were here, and that it was just as arid as it is now. They wouldn't try farming in a place where iron oxide abounds."

"Spinach?"

"You don't know a lot about farming, do you?" asked Jim.

"I saw a cow once."

"That does not qualify you as an expert on farming."

"I know one about the farmer's daughter, and—"

"Not even an expert on dirt farming," continued Jim. "Nope, Barney, we aren't even close."

Barney checked the book once more and scratched his nose.

"How about that eighty-four cycle supply," asked Jim.

"It's eighty-four, all right. From the Martian habit of using twelve as a base, I've calculated the number to be eighty-four."

"Diddle that, too," suggested Jim.

"O.K.," said Barney. "It doesn't take a lot to crank that one around from zero to about fifteen thousand c.p.s. Here she goes!"

Barney took the main dial of the beat-frequency oscillator and began to crank it around the scale. He went up from eighty-four to the top of the dial and then returned. No effect. Then he passed through eighty-four and started down toward zero.

He hit sixty cycles and the jackpot at the same time!

At exactly sixty cycles, a light near the wall dimmed visibly. The wallpaper scorched and burst into a smoldering flame on a wall opposite the dimmed light.

Barney removed the BFO from the vicinity of sixty cycles and Jim extinguished the burning wallpaper.

"Now we're getting somewhere," said Barney.

"This is definitely some sort of weapon," said Jim. "She's not very efficient right now, but we can find out why and then we'll have something hot."

"What for?" asked Barney. "Nobody hates anybody any more."

"Unless the birds who made this thing necessary return," said Jim soberly. His voice was ominous. "We know that only one race of Martians existed, and they were all amicable. I suspect an inimical race from outer space—"

"Could be. Some of the boys are talking about an expedition to Centauri right now. We could have had a visitor from somewhere during the past."

"If you define eternity as the time required for everything to happen once, I agree. In the past or in the future, we have or will be visited by a super race. It may have happened six thousand years ago."

"Did you notice that the electric light is not quite in line with the axis of the tube?" asked Barney.

"Don't turn it any closer," said Jim. "In fact, I'd turn it away before we hook it up again."

"There she is. Completely out of line with the light. Now shall we try it again?"

"Go ahead."

Barney turned the BFO gingerly, and at sixty cycles the thing seemed quite sane. Nothing happened. "Shall I swing it around?"

"I don't care for fires as a general rule," said Jim. "Especially in my own home. Turn it gently, and take care that you don't focus the tube full on that electric light."

Barney moved the tube slightly, and then with a cessation of noise, the clock on the wall stopped abruptly. The accustomed ticking had not been noticed by either man, but the unaccustomed lack-of-ticking became evident at once. Barney shut off the BFO immediately and the two men sat down to a head-scratching session.

"She's good for burning wallpaper, dimming electric lights, and stopping clocks," said Barney. "Any of which you could do without a warehouse full of cockeyed electrical equipment. Wonder if she'd stop anything more powerful than a clock."

"I've got a quarter-horse motor here. Let's wind that up and try it."

The motor was installed on a bench nearby, and the experiment was tried again. At sixty cycles the motor groaned to a stop, and the windings began to smolder. But at the same time the big tube began to exhibit the signs of strain. Meters raced up their scales once more, reached the stops and bent. Barney shut off the motor, but the strains did not stop in the tube. The apparent overload increased linearly and finally the lights went out all over the neighborhood once more.

"Wonderful," said Barney through the darkness. "As a weapon, this thing is surpassed by everything above a fly swatter."

"We might be able to cook a steak with it—if it would take the terrific overload," said Jim. "Or we could use it as an insect exterminator."

"We'd do better by putting the insect on an anvil and hitting it firmly with a five-pound hammer," said Barney. "Then we'd only have the anvil and hammer to haul around. This thing is like hauling a fifty-thousand-watt radio transmitter around. Power supplies, BFO, tube, meters, tools, and a huge truck full of spare fuses for the times when we miss the insect. Might be good for a central heating system."

"Except that a standard electric unit is more reliable and considerably less complicated. You'd have to hire a corps of engineers to run the thing."

The lights went on again, and the attendant in the substation screwed the blow-point control tighter. He didn't know it, but his level was now above the rating for his station. But had he known it he might not have cared. At least, his station was once more in operation.

"Well," said Barney, getting up from the table, "what have we missed?"

Altas said: "Now your unit is operating at its correct level. But, son, you've missed one thing. It is far from efficient. Those two leads must be isolated from one another. Coupling from one to the other will lead to losses."

"Gosh," said Than, "I didn't know that."

"No, for some reason the books assume that the tower engineer has had considerable experience in the art. Take it from me, son, there are a lot of things that are not in the books. Now isolate those leads from one another and we'll go on."

"While you're thinking," said Jim, "I'm going to lockstitch these cables together. It'll make this thing less messy." Jim got a roll of twelve-cord from the cabinet and began to bind the many supply leads into a neat cable.

Barney watched until the job was finished, and then said: "Look, chum, let's try that electric-light trick again."

They swung the tube around until it was in the original position, and turned the juice on. Nothing happened.

Barney looked at Jim, and then reached out and pointed the big tube right at the electric light.

Nothing happened.

"Check your anode voltages again."

"All O.K."

"How about that aligning job?"

Barney fiddled with the alignment screws for minutes, but his original setting seemed to be valid.

"Back to normal," said Barney. "Rip out your cabling."

"Huh?"

"Sure. You did something. I don't know what. But rip it out and fan out the leads. There is something screwy in the supply lines. I've been tied up on that one before; this thing looks like electronics, as we agree, and I've had occasion to remember coupling troubles."

"All right," said Jim, and he reluctantly ripped out his lock-stitching. He fanned the leads and they tried it again.

Obediently the light dimmed and the wallpaper burned.

"Here we go again," said Jim, killing the circuits and reaching for a small rug to smother the fire. "No wonder the Martians had this thing out in the middle of the desert. D'ye suppose that they were trying to find out how it works, too?"

"Take it easier this time and we'll fan the various leads," said Barney. "There's something tricky about the lead placement."

"Half power," announced Barney. "Now, let's get that sixty cycles."

The light dimmed slightly and a sheet of metal placed in front of the tube became slightly warm to the touch. The plate stopped the output of the tube, for the wallpaper did not scorch. Jim began to take supply line after supply line from the bundle of wiring. About halfway through the mess he hit the critical lead, and immediately the light went out completely, and the plate grew quite hot.

"Stop her!" yelled Barney.

"Why?"

"How do we know what we're overloading this time?"

"Do we care?"

"Sure. Let's point this thing away from that light. Then we can hop it up again and try it at full power."

"What do you want to try?"

"This energy-absorption thing."

"Wanna burn out my motor?"

"Not completely. This dingbat will stop a completely mechanical gadget like a clock. It seems to draw power from electric lights. It stops electromechanical power. I wonder just how far it will go toward absorbing power. And also I want to know where the power goes."

The tube was made to stop the clock again. The motor groaned under the load put upon it by the tube. Apparently the action of the tube was similar to a heavy load being placed on whatever its end happened to point to. Barney picked up a small metal block and dropped it over the table.

"Want to see if it absorbs the energy of a falling object—Look at that!"

The block fell until it came inside of the influence of the tube. Then it slowed in its fall and approached the table slowly. It did not hit the table, it touched and came to rest.

"What happens if we wind up a spring and tie it?" asked Jim.

They tried it. Nothing happened.

"Works on kinetic energy, not potential energy," said Barney.

He picked up a heavy hammer and tried to hit the table. "Like swinging a club through a tub of water," he said.

"Be a useful gadget for saving the lives of people who are falling," said Jim thoughtfully.

"Oh, sure. Put it on a truck and rush it out to the scene of the suicide."

"No. How about people jumping out of windows on account of fires? How about having one of the things around during a flier-training course? Think of letting a safe down on one of these beams, or taking a piano from the fifth floor of an apartment building."

"The whole apartment full of furniture could be pitched out of a window," said Barney.

"Mine looks that way now," said Jim, "and we've only moved a couple of times. No, Barney, don't give 'em any ideas."

Jim picked up the hammer and tried to hit the table. Then, idly, he swung the hammer in the direction of the tube's end.

Barney gasped. In this direction there was no resistance. Jim's swing continued, and the look on Jim's face indicated that he was trying to brake the swing in time to keep from hitting the end of the tube. But it seemed as though he were trying to stop an avalanche. The swing continued on and on and finally ended when the hammer head contacted the end of the tube.

There was a burst of fire. Jim swung right on through, whirling around off balance and coming to a stop only when he fell to the floor. He landed in darkness again. The burst of fire emanated from the insulation as it flamed under the heat of extreme overload.

This time the lights were out all over Lincoln Head. The whole city was in complete blackout!

Candles were found, and they inspected the tube anxiously. It seemed whole. But the hammer head was missing. The handle was cut cleanly, on an optically perfect surface.

Where the hammer head went, they couldn't say. But on the opposite wall there was a fracture in the plaster that Jim swore hadn't been there before. It extended over quite an area, and after some thought, Barney calculated that if the force of Jim's hammer blow had been evenly distributed over that area on the wall, the fracturing would have been just about that bad.

"A weapon, all right," said Barney.

"Sure. All you have to do is to shoot your gun right in this end and the force is dissipated over quite an area out of that end. In the meantime you blow out all of the powerhouses on the planet. If a hammer blow can raise such merry hell, what do you think the output of a sixteen-inch rifle would do? Probably stop the planet in its tracks. D'ye know what I think?"

"No, do you?"

"Barney, I think that we aren't even close as to the operation and use of this device."

"For that decision, Jim, you should be awarded the Interplanetary Award for Discovery and Invention—posthumously!"

"So what do we do now?"

"Dunno. How soon does this lighting situation get itself fixed?"

"You ask me.... I don't know either."

"Well, let's see what we've found so far."

"That's easy," said Jim. "It might be a weapon, but it don't weap. We might use it for letting elevators down easy, except that it would be a shame to tie up a room full of equipment when the three-phase electric motor is so simple. We could toast a bit of bread, but the electric toaster has been refined to a beautiful piece of breakfast furniture that doesn't spray off and scorch the wallpaper. We could use it to transmit hammer blows, or to turn out electric lights, but both of those things have been done very simply; one by means of sending the hammerer to the spot, and the other by means of turning the switch. And then in the last couple of cases, there is little sense in turning out a light by short circuiting the socket and blowing all the fuses."

"That is the hard way," smiled Barney. "Like hitting a telephone pole to stop the car, or cutting the wings off a plane to return it to the ground."

"So we have a fairly lucid book that describes the entire hook-up of the thing except what it's for. It gives not only the use of this device, but also variations and replacements. Could we figure it out by sheer deduction?"

"I don't see how. The tower is in the midst of the Red Desert. There is nothing but sand that assays high in iron oxide between Canalopsis, at the junction of the Grand Canal and Lincoln Head. Might be hid, of course, just as this one was, and we'll send out a crew of expert sub-sand explorers with under-surface detectors to cover the ground for a few hundred miles in any direction from the place where we found this. Somehow, I doubt that we'll find much."

"And how do you ... ah, there's the lights again ... deduce that?" asked Jim.

"This gadget is or was of importance to the Martians. Yet in the Temple of Science and Industry at Canalopsis, there is scant mention of the towers."

"Not very much, hey?"

"Very little, in fact. Of course the pictographs on the Temple at Canalopsis shows one tower between what appear two cities. Wavy lines run from one city to the tower and to the other city. Say! I'll bet a cooky that this is some sort of signaling device!"

"A beam transmitter?" asked Jim skeptically. "Seems like a lot of junk for just signaling. Especially when such a swell job can be done with standard radio equipment. A good civilization—such as the Martians must have had—wouldn't piddle around with relay stations between two cities less than a couple of thousand miles apart. With all the juice this thing can suck, they'd be more than able to hang a straight broadcast station and cover halfway around the planet as ground-wave area. What price relay station?"

"Nevertheless, I'm going to tinker up another one of these and see if it is some sort of signaling equipment."

The door opened and Christine Baler entered. She waved a newspaper before her brother's eyes and said: "Boy, have you been missing it!"

"What?" asked Barney.

"Pixies or gremlins loose in Lincoln Head."

"Huh-huh. Read it," said Jim.

"Just a bunch of flash headlines. Fire on Manley Avenue. Three planes had to make dead-tube landings in the center of the city; power went dead for no good reason for about ten minutes. Façade of the City Hall caved in. Power plants running wild all over the place. Ten thousand dollars' worth of electrical equipment blown out. Automobiles stalled in rows for blocks."

Jim looked at Barney. "Got a bear by the tail," he said.

"Could be," admitted Barney.

"Are you two blithering geniuses going to work all night?" asked Christine.

"Nope. We're about out of ideas. Except the one that Barney had about the gadget being some sort of signaling system."

"Why don't you fellows call Don Channing? He's the signaling wizard of the Solar System."

"Sure, call Channing. Every time someone gets an idea, everyone says, 'Call Channing!' He gets called for everything from Boy Scout wigwag ideas to super-cyclotronic-electron-stream beams to contact the outer planets. Based upon the supposition that people will eventually get there, of course."

"Well?"

"Well, I ... we, I mean ... found this thing and we're jolly well going to tinker it out. In spite of the fact that it seems to bollix up everything from electric lights to moving gears. I think we're guilty of sabotage. Façade of the City Hall, et cetera. Barney, how long do you think it will take to tinker up another one of these?"

"Few hours. They're doggoned simple things in spite of the fact that we can't understand them. In fact, I'm of the opinion that the real idea would be to make two; one with only the front end for reception, one for the rear end for transmission, and the one we found for relaying. That's the natural bent, I believe."

"Could be. Where are you going to cut them?"

"The transmitter will start just before the cathode and the receiver will end just after the ... uh, cathode."

"Huh?"

"Obviously the cathode is the baby that makes with the end product. She seems to be a total intake from the intake end and a complete output from the opposite end. Right?"

"Right, but it certainly sounds like heresy."

"I know," said Barney thoughtfully, "but the thing is obviously different from anything that we know today. Who knows how she works?"

"I give up."

Christine, who had been listening in an interested manner, said: "You fellers are the guys responsible for the ruckus that's been going on all over Lincoln Head?"

"I'm afraid so."

"Well, brother warlocks, unless you keep your activities under cover until they're worth mentioning, you'll both be due for burning at the stake."

"O.K., Chris," said Jim. "We'll not let it out."

"But how are you going to tinker up that transmitter-relay-receiver system?"

"We'll take it from here to Barney's place across the avenue and into his garage. That should do it."

"O.K., but now I'm going to bed."

"Shall we knock off, too?" asked Jim.

"Yup. Maybe we'll dream a good thought."

"So long then. We'll leave the mess as it is. No use cleaning up now, we'll only have to mess it up again tomorrow with the same junk."

"And I'll have that—or those—other systems tinkered together by tomorrow noon. That's a promise," said Barney. "And you," he said to Christine, "will operate the relay station."

Altas said to Than: "Now that your system is balanced properly, and we have proved the worth of this tube as a replacement, we shall take it to the roof and install it. The present tube is about due for retirement."

"I've done well, then?" asked Than.

"Considering all, you've done admirably. But balancing the device in the tower, and hooked into the circuit as an integral part is another thing. Come, Than. We shall close the line for an hour whilst replacing the tube."

"Is that permissible?"

"At this time of the night the requirements are small. No damage will be done; they can get along without us for an hour. In fact, at this time of night, only the people who are running the city will know that we are out of service. And it is necessary that the tube be maintained at full capability. We can not chance a weakened tube; it might fail when it is needed the most."

Than carried the tube to the top of the tower, and Altas remained to contact the necessary parties concerning the shut-off for replacement purposes. He followed Than to the top after a time and said: "Now disconnect the old tube and put it on the floor. We shall replace the tube immediately, but it will be an hour before it is properly balanced again."

It was not long before Than had the tube connected properly. "Now," said Altas, "turn it on one-tenth power and we shall align it."

"Shall I use the meters?"

"I think it best. This requires perfect alignment now. We've much power and considerable distance, and any losses will create great amounts of heat."

"All right," said Than. He left the tower top to get the meters.

Barney Carroll spoke into a conveniently placed microphone. "Are you ready?" he asked.

"Go ahead," said Christine.

"We're waiting," said Jim.

"You're the bird on the transmitter," said Barney to Jim. "*You* make with the juice."

Power rheostats were turned up gingerly, until Jim shouted to stop. His shout was blotted out by cries from the other two. They met in Barney's place to confer.

"What's cooking?" asked Jim.

"The meters are all going crazy in my end," said Barney. "I seem to be sucking power out of everything in line with my tube."

"The so-called relay station is firing away at full power and doing nothing but draining plenty of power from the line," complained Christine.

"And on my end, I was beginning to scorch the wallpaper again. I don't understand it. With no receiver-end, how can I scorch wallpaper?"

"Ask the Martians. They know."

"You ask 'em. What shall we do, invent a time machine and go back sixty centuries?"

"Wish we could," said Barney. "I'd like to ask the bird that left this textbook why they didn't clarify it more."

"Speaking of Don Channing again," said Jim, "I'll bet a hat that one of his tube-replacement manuals for the big transmitters out on Venus Equilateral do not even mention that the transmitter requires a receiver before it is any good. We think we're modern. We are, and we never think that some day some poor bird will try to decipher our technical works. Why, if Volta himself came back and saw the most perfect machine ever invented—the transformer—he'd shudder. No connection between input and output, several kinds of shorted loops of wire; and instead of making a nice simple electromagnet, we short the lines of force and on top of that we use a lot of laminations piled on top of one another instead of a nice, soft iron core. We completely short the input, et cetera, but how do we make with a gadget like that?"

"I know. We go on expecting to advance. We forget the simple past. Remember the lines of that story: 'How does one chip the flint to make the best arrowhead?' I don't know who wrote it any more than I know how to skin a boar, but we do get on without making arrowheads or skinning boars or trimming birch-bark canoes."

"All right, but there's still this problem."

"Remember how we managed to align this thing? I wonder if it might not take another alignment to make it work as a relay."

"Could be," said Jim. "I'll try it. Christine, you work these screws at the same time we do, and make the current come out as low as we can."

They returned to their stations and began to work on the alignment screws. Jim came out first on the receiver. Christine was second on the transmitter, while Barney fumbled for a long time with the relay tube.

Then Christine called: "Fellows, my meter readings are climbing up again. Shall I diddle?"

"Wait a minute," said Barney. "That means I'm probably taking power out of that gadget you have in there. Leave 'em alone."

He fiddled a bit more, and then Jim called: "Whoa, Nellie. Someone just lost me a millimeter. She wound up on the far end."

"Hm-m-m," said Barney, "so we're relaying."

"Go ahead," said Jim. "I've got a ten-ampere meter on here now."

Barney adjusted his screws some more.

"Wait a minute," said Jim. "I'm going to shunt this meter up to a hundred amps."

"What?" yelled Barney.

"Must you yell?" asked Christine ruefully. "These phones are plenty uncomfortable without some loudmouthed bird screaming."

"Sorry, but a hundred amps... *whoosh*! What have we got here, anyway?"

"Yeah," said Christine. "I was about to say that my input meter is running wild again."

"Gone?"

"Completely. You shouldn't have hidden it behind that big box. I didn't notice it until just now, but she's completely gone."

"I'll be over. I think we've got something here."

An hour passed, during which nothing of any great importance happened. By keying the transmitter tube, meters in the receiver tube were made to read in accordance. Then they had another conclave.

"Nothing brilliant," said Jim. "We could use super-output voice amplifiers and yell halfway across the planet if we didn't have radio. We can radio far better than this cockeyed system of signaling."

"We might cut the power."

"Or spread out quite a bit. I still say, however, that this is no signaling system."

"It works like one."

"So can a clothesline be made to serve as a transmitter of intelligence. But it's prime function is completely different."

"S'pose we have a super-clothesline here?" asked Christine.

"The way that hammer felt last night, I'm not too sure that this might not be some sort of tractor beam," said Jim.

"Tractor beams are mathematically impossible."

"Yeah, and they proved conclusively that a bird cannot fly," said Jim. "That was before they found the right kind of math. Up until Clerk Maxwell's time, radio was mathematically impossible. Then he discovered the electromagnetic equations, and we're squirting signals across the Inner System every day. And when math and fact do not agree, which changes?"

"The math. Galileo proved that. Aristotle said that a heavy stone will fall faster. Then Galileo changed the math of that by heaving a couple of boulders off the Leaning Tower. But what have we here?"

"Has anyone toyed with the transmission of power?"

"Sure. A lot of science-fiction writers have their imaginary planets crisscrossed with transmitted power. Some broadcast it, some have it beamed to the consumer. When they use planes, they have the beam coupled to an object-finder so as to control the direction of the beam. I prefer the broadcasting, myself. It uncomplicates the structure of the tale."

"I mean actually?"

"Oh, yes. But the losses are terrific. Useful power transmission is a minute percentage of the total output of the gadget. Absolutely impractical, especially when copper and silver are so plentiful to string along the scenery on steel towers. No good."

"But look at this cockeyed thing. Christine puts in a couple of hundred amps; I take them off my end. Believe it or not, the output meter at my end was getting a lot more soup than I was pouring in."

"And my gadget was not taking anything to speak of," said Barney.

"Supposing it was a means of transmitting power. How on Mars did they use a single tower there in the middle of the Red Desert? We know there was a Martian city at Canalopsis, and another one not many miles from Lincoln Head. Scribbled on the outer cover of this book is the legend: 'Tower Station, Red Desert,' and though the Martians didn't call this the 'Red Desert, the terminology will suffice for nomenclature."

"Well?" asked Jim.

"You notice they did not say: 'Station No. 1,' or '3' or '7.' That means to me that there was but one."

"Holy Smoke! Fifteen hundred miles with only one station? On Mars the curvature of ground would put such a station below the electrical horizon—" Jim thought that one over for a minute and then said: "Don't tell me they bent the beam?"

"Either they did that or they heated up the sand between," said Barney cryptically. "It doesn't mind going through nonconducting walls, but a nice, fat ground ... blooey, or I miss my guess. That'd be like grounding a high line."

"You're saying that they did bend—*Whoosh*, again!"

"What was that alignment problem? Didn't we align the deflecting anodes somehow?"

"Yeah, but you can't bend the output of a cathode-ray tube externally of the deflection plates."

"But this is not electron-beam stuff," objected Barney. "This is as far ahead of cathode-ray tubes as they are ahead of the Indian signal drum or the guy who used to run for twenty-four miles from Ghent to Aix."

"That one was from Athens to Sparta," explained Christine, "the Ghent to Aix journey was a-horseback, and some thousand-odd years after."

"Simile's still good," said Barney. "There's still a lot about this I do not understand."

"A masterpiece of understatement, if I ever heard one," laughed Jim. "Well, let's work on it from that angle. Come on, gang, to horse!"

"Now," said Altas, "you will find that the best possible efficiency is obtained when the currents in these two resistances are equal and opposite in direction. That floats the whole tube on the system, and makes it possible to run the tube without any external power source. It requires a starter-source for aligning and for standby service, and for the initial surge: then it is self-sustaining. Also the in-phase voltage can not better be obtained than by exciting the phasing anode with some of the main-line power. That must always be correctly phased. We now need the frequency generator no longer, and by increasing the power rheostat to full, the tube will take up the load. Watch the meters, and when they read full power, you may throw the cut-over switch and make the tube self-sustaining. Our tower will then be in perfect service, and you and I may return to our home below."

Than performed the operations, and then they left, taking the old tube with them.

And on Terra, Sargon of Akkad watched ten thousand slaves carry stone for one of his public buildings. He did not know that on one of the stars placed in the black bowl of the evening sky for his personal benefit, men were flinging more power through the air than the total output of all of his slaves combined. Had he been told, he would have had the teller beheaded for lying because Sargon of Akkad couldn't possibly have understood it—

"You know, we're missing a bet," said Jim. "This in-phase business here. Why shouldn't we hang a bit of the old wall-socket juice in here?"

"That might be the trick," said Barney.

Jim made the connections, and they watched the meters read up and up and up—and from the street below them a rumbling was heard. Smoke issued from a crevasse in the pavement, and then with a roar, the street erupted and a furrow three feet wide and all the way across the street from Jim Baler's residence to Barney Carroll's garage lifted out of the ground. It blew straight up and fell back, and from the bottom of the furrow the smoldering of burned and tortured wiring cast a foul smell.

"*Wham!*" said Barney, looking at the smoking trench. "What was that?"

"I think we'll find that it was the closest connection between our places made by the Electric Co.," said Jim.

"But what have we done?"

"I enumerate," said Christine, counting off on her fingers. "We've blasted in the façade of the City Hall. We've caused a couple of emergency flier-landings within the city limits. We've blown fuses and circuit breakers all the way from here to the main powerhouse downtown. We've stalled a few dozen automobiles. We've torn or burned or cut the end off of one hammer and have fractured the wall with it ... where did that go, anyway, the hammerhead? We've burned wallpaper. We've run our electric bill up to about three hundred dollars, I'll bet. We've bunged up a dozen meters. And now we've ripped up a trench in the middle of the street."

"Somewhere in this set-up, there is a return circuit," said Jim thoughtfully. "We've been taking power out of the line, and I've been oblivious of the fact that a couple of hundred amperes is too high to get out of our power line without trouble. What we've been doing is taking enough soup out of the public utility lines to supply the losses only. The power we've been seeing on our meters is the build-up, recirculated!"

"Huh?"

"Sure. Say we bring an amp in from the outside and shoot it across the street. It goes to the wires and comes back because of some electrical urge in our gadgets here, and then goes across the street in-phase with the original. That makes two amps total crossing our beam. The two come back and we have two plus two. Four come back, and we double again and again until the capability of our device is at saturation. All we have to do is to find the ground-return and hang a load in there. We find the transmitter-load input, and supply that with a generator. Brother, we can beam power all the way from here to Canalopsis on one relay tower!"

Barney looked at his friend. "Could be."

"Darned right. What other item can you think of that fits this tower any better? We've run down a dozen ideas, but this works. We may be arrested for wrecking Lincoln Head, but we'll get out as soon as this dingbat hits the market. Brother, what a find!"

"Fellows, I think you can make your announcement now," smiled Christine. "They won't burn you at the stake if you can bring electric power on a beam of pure nothing. This time you've hit the jackpot!"

It is six thousand Terran Years since Sargon of Akkad held court that was lighted by torch. It is six thousand years, Terran, since Than and Altas replaced the link in a power system that tied their cities together.

It is six thousand years since the beam tower fell into the Red Desert and the mighty system of beamed power became lost as an art. But once again the towers dot the plains, not only of Mars, but of Venus and Terra, too.

And though they are of a language understood by the peoples of three worlds, the manuals of instruction would be as cryptic to Than as his manual was to Barney Carroll and Jim Baler.

People will never learn.